JIM CORBETT

THE MAN-EATER OF CHAMPAWAT
THE MOHAN TIGER

First published by Westland Books, a division of Nasadiya Technologies Private Limited, in 2024

No. 269/2B, First Floor, 'Irai Arul', Vimalraj Street, Nethaji Nagar, Alapakkam Main Road, Maduravoyal, Chennai 600095

Westland and the Westland logo are the trademarks of Nasadiya Technologies Private Limited, or its affiliates.

Text and illustrations copyright © Nasadiya Technologies Private Limited, 2024

This comic is an adaptation of two short stories from *Man-eaters of Kumaon* by Jim Corbett—'The Champawat Man-eater' and 'The Mohan Man-eater'.

ISBN:

10 9 8 7 6 5 4 3 2 1

This is a work of fiction. Names, characters, organisations, places, events and incidents are either products of the author's imagination or used fictitiously.

All rights reserved

Comic Script: Angelin Diana
Art and Corrections: Angelin Diana, Ayantika Roy, Ashiq Shanavas, Dolly Thakrar, Pankaj Deore and Tanisha Tiwari
Lettering: Pooja Padmashali
Art Direction: Angelin Diana
Creative Quality Control: Abhigyan Singh
Creative Producer: Rajeev Tamhankar

Book design by New Media Line Creations, New Delhi

Printed at Parksons Graphics Pvt. Ltd

No part of this book may be reproduced, or stored in a retrieval system, or transmitted in any form or by any means, electronic, mechanical, photocopying, recording, or otherwise, without express written permission of the publisher.

THE MAN-EATER
OF CHAMPAWAT

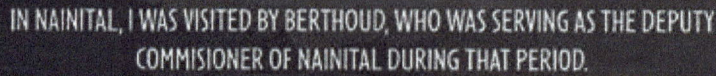

IT WAS NOT UNTIL THE RESCUE PARTY HAD SET OUT SPEEDILY AND RETURNED WITHOUT HER SISTER THAT THE VILLAGERS REALISED THE WOMAN HAD LOST HER POWER OF SPEECH.

THIS WAS THE TALE I HEARD IN THE VILLAGE. AND WHEN I CLIMBED THE PATH TO THE TWO-ROOMED HUT WHERE THE WOMAN WAS ENGAGED IN WASHING CLOTHES, SHE HAD THEN BEEN MUTE FOR TWELVE MONTHS.

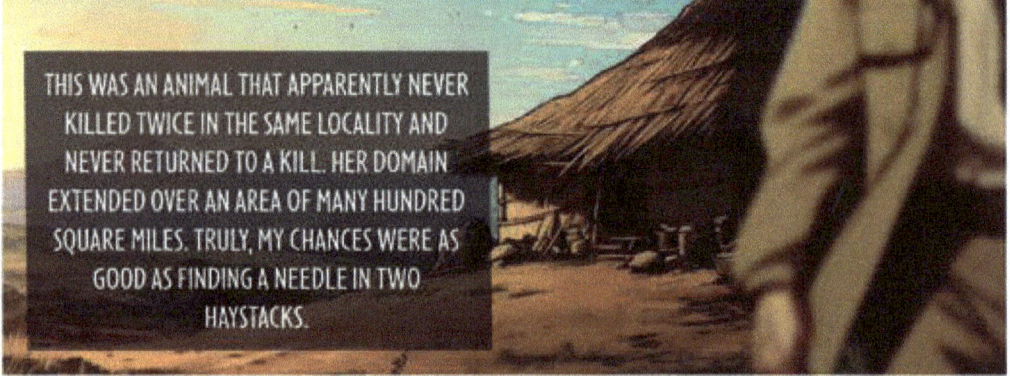

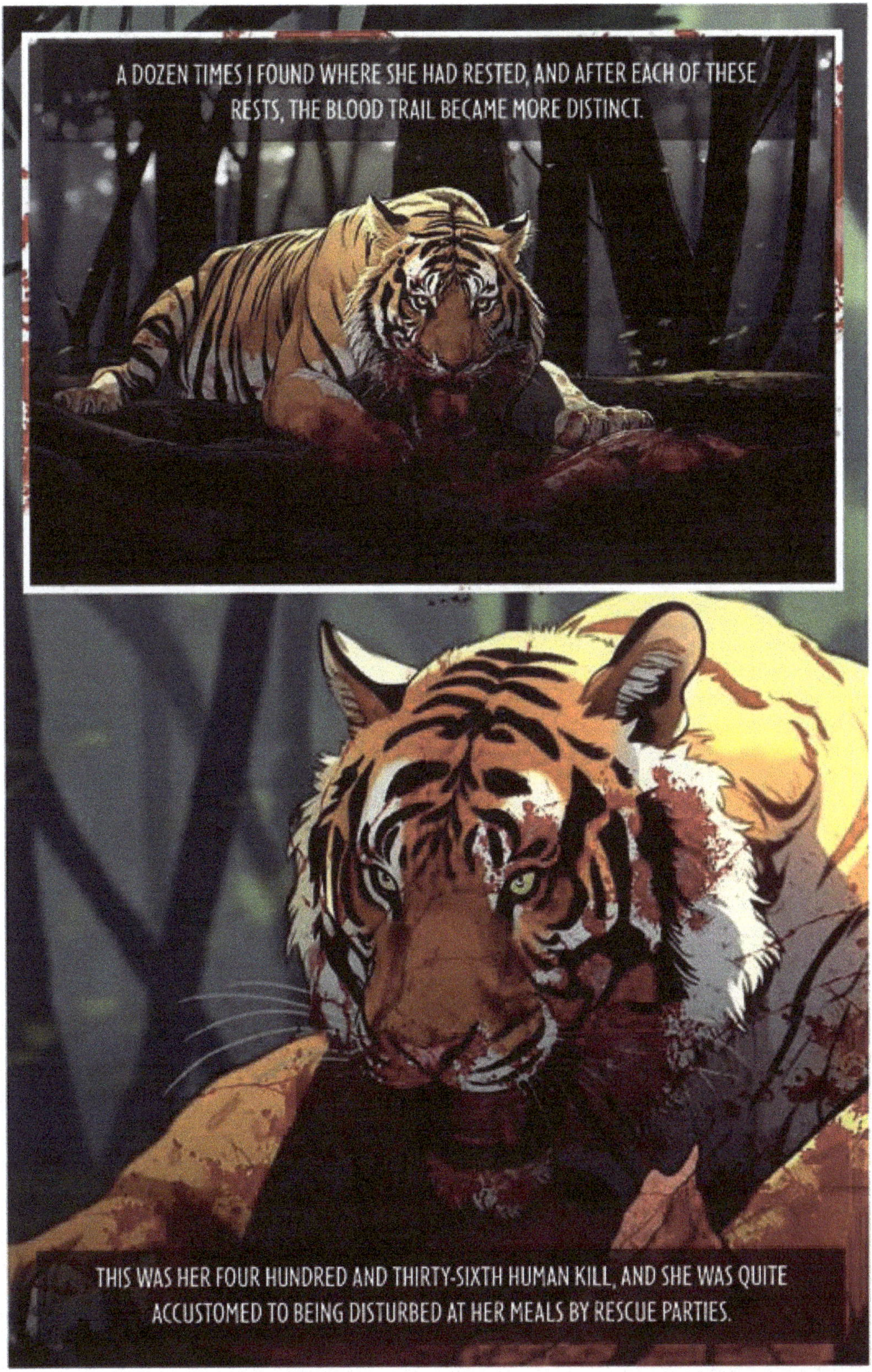

A DOZEN TIMES I FOUND WHERE SHE HAD RESTED, AND AFTER EACH OF THESE RESTS, THE BLOOD TRAIL BECAME MORE DISTINCT.

THIS WAS HER FOUR HUNDRED AND THIRTY-SIXTH HUMAN KILL, AND SHE WAS QUITE ACCUSTOMED TO BEING DISTURBED AT HER MEALS BY RESCUE PARTIES.

PANDEMONIUM BROKE LOOSE ON THE RIDGE. ADDED TO THE FUSILLADE OF GUNS WAS THE WILD BEATING OF DRUMS AND THE SHOUTING OF HUNDREDS OF MEN...

...AND WHEN THE DIN WAS AT ITS WORST, I CAUGHT SIGHT OF THE TIGRESS BOUNDING DOWN A GRASSY SLOPE BETWEEN TWO RAVINES TO MY RIGHT, ABOUT THREE HUNDRED YARDS AWAY.

WHEN I WAS WITHIN TWENTY FEET OF HER, I RAISED THE GUN, AND FOUND TO MY HORROR THAT THERE WAS A GAP OF ABOUT THREE-EIGHTS OF AN INCH BETWEEN THE GUN'S BARRELS AND ITS BREECH-BLOCK.

HOWEVER, I WOULD HAVE TO TAKE THAT RISK. SO, ALIGNING THE GREAT BLOB OF A BEAD THAT DID DUTY AS A SIGHT ON THE TIGRESS'S OPEN MOUTH, I FIRED.

FROM THE MOMENT THE TIGRESS HAD BROKEN COVER IN HER ATTEMPT TO GET THROUGH THE GORGE, I HAD FORGOTTEN THE BEATERS. NOW, A SHOUT SUDDENLY REMINDED ME OF THEIR EXISTENCE.

WHEN THE TIGRESS HAD STOOD ON THE ROCK LOOKING DOWN AT ME, I HAD NOTICED THAT THERE WAS SOMETHING WRONG WITH HER MOUTH...

THE MOHAN TIGER

EIGHTEEN MILES FROM OUR SUMMER HOME IN THE HIMALAYAS, THERE IS A LONG RIDGE. ON ITS UPPER SLOPE THERE IS A LUXURIANT GROWTH OF OAT GRASS; BELOW THIS GRASS THE HILL FALLS STEEPLY AWAY IN A SERIES OF ROCK CLIFFS TO THE KOSI RIVER BELOW.

WHEN THE PEOPLE FROM THE VILLAGE REACHED THE SITE, THEY SAW THE INJURED WOMAN LYING IN A SWOON.

AND THEY SAW SPLASHES OF BLOOD ON THE LEDGE.

ALL THAT THE TIGER HAD LEFT OF THE BRAVE YOUNG GIRL WHO HAD VOLUNTEERED TO STAY WITH HER INJURED COMPANION WERE A FEW BITS OF FLESH AND HER TORN AND BLOOD-STAINED CLOTHES.

Rustle

I AM A LIGHT SLEEPER, AND TWO OR THREE HOURS LATER, I AWOKE TO THE SOUND OF AN ANIMAL MOVING ABOUT IN THE JUNGLE.

EVENTUALLY, THE NIGHT PROVED TO BE UNEVENTFUL. AFTER AN EARLY BREAKFAST, I SENT FOUR MEN DOWN TO MOHAN TO BRING UP THE TWO BUFFALOES.

MEANWHILE, I VENTURED TO THE SITE WHERE THE TIGER HAD ATTACKED AND KILLED THE WOMAN.

THE RAIN WASHED AWAY THE HAZE AND DUST, LEAVING A BRILLIANTLY CLEAR MORNING. EVERY LEAF AND BLADE OF GRASS SPARKLED IN THE NEWLY RISEN SUN.

THE RAIN SOFTENED THE SURFACE OF THE ROAD, MAKING IT AN OPPORTUNE TIME TO SEARCH FOR TIGER TRACKS.

AT THE DAMP SPOT ON THE ROAD, CLOSE TO THE BUFFALO'S LOCATION, I FOUND FRESH PUG MARKS HEADING TOWARDS THE RIDGE.

I CLIMBED A ROCK TO GET A BETTER VIEW OF THE AREA AND SPOTTED THE NOW DEAD BUFFALO BELOW IN THE THICK UNDERGROWTH.

TIGERS GUARD THEIR KILLS, SO I SUSPECTED THIS ONE WAS NEARBY, HIDDEN IN THE DENSE JUNGLE.

MY THROAT IRRITATED ME, AND I TRIED TO SUPPRESS A COUGH TO AVOID ALERTING THE TIGER.

IN DESPERATION, I ATTEMPTED TO MIMIC THE LANGUR'S ALARM CALL TO SOOTHE MY THROAT. IT WORKED, BUT I FEARED THE TIGER MIGHT HAVE HEARD.

I IMAGINED THAT THE TIGER WAS CROUCHING, READY TO POUNCE THE MOMENT I REVEALED MYSELF.

I NOTICED THAT THE SUN WAS SHINING ON THE GRASS, MAKING IT TOO HOT FOR THE TIGER TO STAY PUT.

IF I WANTED TO SEE THE TIGER'S POSITION, I HAD TO APPROACH CAREFULLY, BUT I COULDN'T MAKE A SOUND.

> I HAD TO AVOID COUGHING OR MAKING ANY NOISE THAT COULD REVEAL MY PRESENCE.

> I MOVED EVEN MORE CAUTIOUSLY, MAKING SURE NOT TO DISTURB A SINGLE BLADE OF GRASS.

> SUCCESS! THE TIGER WAS LYING DOWN, NOT CROUCHING TO SPRING AT ME.

WITH THE TIGER RESTING, I LINED UP MY SHOT, PRESSING THE TRIGGER SOFTLY AND SILENTLY RELEASING THE SAFETY-CATCH.

BANG!

THE HEAVY BULLET STRUCK THE TIGER'S FOREHEAD, KILLING HIM INSTANTLY.

THE TIGER'S MAN-EATING BEHAVIOUR WAS LIKELY A RESULT OF HIS OWN PAIN AND SUFFERING.

IN THE END, HE WAS A VICTIM TOO.

The End

www.ingramcontent.com/pod-product-compliance
Lightning Source LLC
LaVergne TN
LVHW061626070526
838199LV00070B/6595